Fugar

A Holiday Experience

by Nicole Julius & Paul Julius

HSR HUB PUBLISHING

First published in Great Britain in 2018 by HSR HUB LIMITED

A CIP catalogue record for this book is available from the British Library upon request.

ISBN: 978-1-9164832-0-0

Dedication

With love and affection to my grandma Titi-Maria, for inspiring it

And to my mum, for making everything possible

NJ

"Emmie! Emmie!" called mum.

"Taxi's here," she added in her usual warm voice.

"Hurry up, we wouldn't want to be late for our flight."

"I'm coming mum!" I yelled back excitedly. Quickly, I rushed to wear my floral sandals and grabbed my Frozen trolley suitcase. It feels a little light for a week's vacation. I wondered whether I'd packed everything? *No time to check. I've got to go.*

"I'm ready!" I called as I hurried down the stairs. I spotted mum wheeling a giant blue stripy suitcase in one hand. She held Ossie my little baby brother in the other.

We gathered around the front door to leave the house. *Click! Click!* Dad turned the key to lock the door. Mum led the way to the taxi. Our luggage was nicely organised into the boot of the car. I sat with Ossie in the back, he was strapped to the child seat while we waited for dad.

FROZEN

Dad was about to enter the taxi when mum asked "did you pick up our passports?".

"Yes," answered dad. Flashing all four passports with a broad smile.

The driver drove all the way to the airport. Lost in thoughts, I was as quiet as a mouse. I couldn't stop wondering, imagining what Africa would be like. What Nigeria would be like. Dad said we are going to Nigeria to visit Titi-Maria.

Titi-Maria is my grandma. My dad's mum. She lives in a small village called Fugar. I was once told that people in the village live in huts made out of straws. Just like in the story of the 'three little piggies and the big bad wolf'. I couldn't wait to stay in one of those huts. I wondered if I huffed and puffed, I could blow a house down. How mischievous, I smiled.

"Heathrow Airport," announced the taxi driver.

"That is seventy pounds please," he added.

Dad handed over the fare and went to look for one of those airport trolleys. He wheeled one over and loaded our luggage. Gosh! I didn't think we needed so much stuff. Mum had bought lots of presents to give my uncles, aunties and cousins. She says it's tradition to give presents when you go and visit family or friends in Nigeria.

A Holiday Experience

I have ten aunties and uncles, and then there's cousins Jason, Joseph and Derek. I can't wait to meet them all.

As we made our way to the airport entrance, mum murmured loud enough for us to hear "our flight leaves in two hours". We started to hurry. We wouldn't want to miss our flight now, would we?

∞ ∞ ∞

The flight was a very quiet one. Probably because it was a night flight and almost everyone on board was asleep. Ossie curled up on mum's laps looking very comfortable while he slept. Mum was also fast asleep. Dad was reading The Punch newspaper. He said he wanted to catch up on the latest news before we landed.

I couldn't sleep. All the excitement of meeting my extended family for the first time kept me wide awake. I was also a bit anxious. I didn't know what to expect.

I tried to distract myself by watching a movie. I flicked through the channels, it was quite difficult to find a movie that I hadn't already seen. I'll settle for 'high school musicals 2', I reluctantly decided.

We arrived at Murtala Mohammed Airport, Lagos. The plane touched down but before the Captain could announce 'welcome to Lagos', everyone jumped out of their seats. Scuffling to get their luggage from the cabinets above, I wondered why everyone was in such a rush.

"Give me ja re," a middle-aged woman snapped in pidgin English at the man in front of her.

"I beg o, wey tin," the man snapped back. They argued till the Captain was ready to let us off the plane.

It was extremely slow getting off the plane. There was a long queue of passengers in front of us, and it seemed like we were going to be there forever. Ossie started to get a bit agitated. Mum tried to keep him calm by softly singing into his ears.

"You can have this Ossie." I offered, handing him one of my custard cream biscuits.

Ossie grabbed the biscuit from my hand straight into his mouth.

"Thanks Emmie," said mum with relief.

She turned to Ossie "you know you're not allowed biscuit before breakfast," she said teasingly.

"That's right little man," butted in dad. Ossie didn't seem to care, he was busy enjoying his sugary treat.

FROZEN

At last, it was our turn to alight. The warm humid air of Lagos blew on my face as I stepped off the plane. It felt wonderful. *This is great!* I sighed.

Uncle Odior was already waiting at the arrival.

"It's so good to see you Emmie," he said lifting me off my feet. I gave him a big teddy bear hug.

"It's great to see you too uncle," I replied giggling.

He gently put me down and held his arms out to embrace Ossie. Ossie looked puzzled at first, he waited a few minutes before reacting. He jumped onto uncle Odior and chuckled. Then he wrapped his chubby little hands around uncle Odior's neck and gave him a long warm hug.

"Where are you parked?" interrupted dad.

"Over at the front," replied uncle Odior, holding tightly onto Ossie.

"We better get moving before the morning traffic starts," advised mum.

∞ ∞ ∞

It was a short journey from the airport to uncle Odior's house. But it took longer to get there because we did get stucked in the morning peak hour traffic.

I was unusually quiet as the traffic slowly moved. I leaned against the car window, observing the street and pondering on everything I saw. Dad, mum and uncle Odior were busy chit chatting while Ossie had fallen asleep, again. Suddenly, a lady carrying a tray of chips on her head appeared out of the blue.

"Plantain chips, fifty naira! Plantain chips, fifty naira!" She chanted, dangling a pack of plantain chips in front of my window.

"What are those?" I asked curiously.

"They are plantain chips," blurted uncle Odior, signaling over the plantain chips seller to his side of the window.

"Oga, how many make I bring?" said the plantain chips seller, shoveling a bunch of plantain chips through the window.

"Oga, pure water nko?" offered another hawker who mysteriously appeared from behind the plantain chips seller.

"No pure water," said uncle Odior, pulling out his wallet from his trouser back pocket. He handed over cash to the plantain chips seller. She gave him some change and left happy as a bee.

Shortly afterwards we arrived at uncle Odior's house.

My uncles, aunties and cousins were already waiting, "welcome o, ekabo, ara ilu oyinbo," they chanted.

Our first day in Nigeria turned out to be a very long and busy day. We had many guests trooping in to see us. I was exhausted and so was mum by the look of it. Ossie seemed to be having fun. Spoilt with many choices of hands to carry him around; it was like a game of pass the parcel.

Dad was also having a blast. "We leave for Fugar in the morning," I overheard him say to one of my uncles. Fugar is in Edo State, mid-western Nigeria. It is where Titi-Maria lives. Dad said it's a long drive from uncle Odior's house to Fugar. He also said there are many beautiful scenes and lots of interesting things to see on the way. I probably wouldn't need my ipad but I better make sure mum packs enough nibbles for the trip.

We woke up very early the next day. The taxi was waiting outside. It was a yellow cab with black stripes. The driver sat patiently inside until he saw us appear. Then he came out to meet us "ekaro" he greeted, good morning. He turned to me with a bony smile "you dey enjoy Naija?" he asked. Naija is the nickname for Nigeria. Yes, I nodded.

It was a bumpier ride through the busy streets of Lagos. It was barely 7:30am, and the people were already out and about. The hawkers had started to roam the streets carrying trays of goods on their heads. I leaned against the window with my chin comfortably resting on crossed arms, and began to observe. The bright multi-coloured houses with tall dark gates, none of them made out of straws! A man pushing a wheelbarrow of bottled and square shaped sachet water bags chanting 'pure water! pure water!'. What seemed like an endless line of passengers waiting to board the next B.R.T. bus. Oh! And there's the overloaded Danfo bus trying to overtake our taxi. I was fascinated by it all.

We drove for a while before we arrived at the Ore Motor Park precisely 11:45am. It was a very busy motor park with lots of petty trading. Not surprising, everyone was itching to get out of the car for a comfort break.

The motor park had restaurants, music, craft sales, scrumptiously looking delicacies, and there was my favourite, suya! Oh how I'd longed for the delightful taste of the hot spicy tenderly grilled meat. The spicy aroma filled the air and my tummy started to rumble. "Dad, can I have some suya please," I asked eagerly.

"Sure," replied dad, and we left to get some suya. We bought enough suya and Agege bread for everyone. Dad handed out the suya and bread. For the next few minutes, all you could hear was the ruffling sound of suya paper being unwrapped, followed by the munching.

"Hmm, the suya sweet well, well," said auntie Koko.

"Dem do am well," agreed uncle Odior.

We rode on more jerky roads as we drove further through Benin City and to Auchi. I noticed more people nearby. I saw farms, oil palm plantations, and houses. Mud houses with wooden windows, some with thatched roofs and others with none. I also noticed an unusual looking statue of a man.

"Where are we?" I asked.

"We're at Fugar," answered uncle Odior cheerfully.

"Fugar!" I exclaimed and looked over at mum who flashed a smile at me.

I turned back to the window, I didn't want to miss a thing. Fascinated by the little village, *so this is where dad grew up,* I mumbled to myself. Soon, I'll be meeting Titi-Maria, and I can't wait.

We approached an alley. I could see in the distance a small compound surrounded by red bricked walls.

We entered the compound, it smelt of earth and smoke. Titi-Maria, my grandma was resting on a mat under an orange tree. As soon as she saw us, she rose to meet us. She was beautiful and looked strong in spite of her wrinkled face. She came dancing towards us singing a Fugar song. Her smile was graceful and warm. I ran to meet her.

We unloaded our bags from the taxi. I was excited to give grandma the present I bought her from an antique shop in Sittingbourne. "Open my gift mama" I urged her. She opened the present to reveal a lovely silky red scarf. Titi-Maria smiled and placed her right hand on my head saying "bless you my daughter."

Lunch was served, we had pounded yam and groundnut stew, dad's favourite. After lunch, I went to join the other children playing outside. They were intrigued by me and kept asking questions about England. None of them have travelled out of Fugar before. So the story of my flight from Heathrow to Lagos caught their imagination.

We laughed and played together, chasing butterflies and chickens around the compound. We climbed trees and played ball. It was getting dark when mum called me in for dinner. I didn't realise how hungry and tired I was. I was off to bed straight after.

I woke up to the crow of grandma's hens: *cock-a-doodle-doo! cock-a-doodle-doo!!* Who needs an alarm clock when you've got chickens! I got up, got dressed and brushed my teeth. Titi-Maria was cooking on the charcoal stove outside. She was making breakfast. "Emmie, my daughter, please get me more firewood," she asked pointing to the log pile. "Here's the firewood mama," I said handing Titi-Maria the log. I looked around and spotted mum in the hen house. She was collecting eggs for breakfast so I went over to help. This is fun, we usually get our eggs from Asda or Tesco.

After getting some eggs, we harvested a few tomatoes and thyme. Mum chopped the tomatoes while I grinded the thyme with the mortar and pestle. Titi-Maria poured the chopped tomatoes and grinded thyme into the frying eggs. Moments later, the food was ready and we all had yam and fried eggs for breakfast.

∞ ∞ ∞

At noon, Titi-Maria announced she was going to Ivhiadachi village market.

"Can I come?" I asked. "Of course my daughter."

The village market was a short walk from the house. It was quite a sight! The open market stretched to the end of the long street. The sellers arranged their goods on round metal trays, some in baskets. Some placed their trays on the ground, others carried them on their heads, just like the hawkers in Lagos. It was very noisy. The sellers chatting and scouting for customers. Some women had their toddlers strapped to their backs, just like mum carries Ossie.

"We are going to Ogbeh's stall," said Titi-Maria. Ogbeh is one of Titi-Maria's childhood friends. She sells vegetables, sugar and palm oil in the village market.

"Ogbo, Titi-Maria," greeted Ogbeh in Fugar language.

"Opuno, Ogbeh," responded Titi-Maria.

"Welcome my children," she turned to us and said. Soon, people started coming into Ogbeh's stall to buy foodstuff. I liked watching Ogbeh trade her goods. I even helped customers pack their merchandise in carrier bags to take home. It was time to leave and Ogbeh gave me a jar of 'otopo' as a thank you gift for being helpful at the stall. "This we'll use to eat boiled yam," said dad, admiring the jar of thickened palm oil.

MARKET

We took the bank of the village river route back home. There I saw a single thatched hut sitting in isolation. That seemed rather odd so I decided to ask Titi-Maria all about it when we got home. "You see my daughter, there is more to what the eyes can see," she began and told the touching story of how the infamous prophet was banished by the king.

That night, I pondered on the story of the infamous prophet. I shall have an interesting tale to tell my friends at Grove Park when school resumes.

We travel back to Lagos tomorrow and board an early flight to Heathrow two days after.

∞ ∞ ∞

The next day, I was up before the cock crowed and so was Titi-Maria and everyone else. We leave after breakfast but I didn't want to go. I asked if Titi-Maria could come with us to England. She smiled and said "I am too old for the long journey by air, my daughter. I will be waiting for you to visit me again soon." Then she gave me a gift. It was a necklace made from African beads. I wore it around my neck. I hugged my grandma tightly as we said our final goodbyes.

I watched Titi-Maria through the car window as we drove out of the compound. 'I hope to see you soon mama,' I muttered as I wiped the last drop of tear from my eyes.

Glossary

Agege Bread – A popular Nigerian regular white bread known for its soft, stretchy and chewy texture.

Groundnut Stew – A popular West African soup made from peanut paste.

Naira – The Nigerian currency.

Oga – Used to refer to a 'boss' in Nigeria.

Otopo – A thickened palm oil which is an edible vegetable oil derived from the fruit of oil palms.

Pidgin English – A grammatically simplified means of communication derived from English language spoken in most parts of West Africa.

Plantain Chips – A type of chips that are made by frying slices of unripened plantain which is similar to banana.

Pounded Yam – A popular Nigerian meal made from boiled white yam and pounded in a mortar with three to five foot tall pestle into a smooth textured dough

Suya – Roast African spicy skewered beef popular in Nigeria as a street food.

Authors' Mission

To encourage all children to have the power of literacy.

29778129R00021

Printed in Poland
by Amazon Fulfillment
Poland Sp. z o.o., Wrocław